THE
Snow
Bear

THE
Snow
Bear

by
Miriam Moss

illustrated by
Maggie Kneen

SCHOLASTIC INC.
New York   Toronto   London   Auckland   Sydney
Mexico City   New Delhi   Hong Kong   Buenos Aires

In the silent forest is a clearing
where soft snowflakes fall.

But listen!

There's padding
and pouncing,
and a snowdrift
shivers.

A little white bear
bursts into the clearing.
He looks left and right,
high and low for
his mother.

"Mother! Where are you?" calls the
little white bear. He waits and waits,
but she does not come.
"I will make a snow mother,"
he whispers, "to keep me
company while I wait."
The little white bear sweeps
snow into a mother shape.

But listen!

There's snuffling and swishing
and a deep crunch of snow.
Musk Ox shakes his shaggy coat.

"Let me help," he says.
And he heaves a
heavy mound of snow
with his strong shoulder.

There's stirring
and whirring and a
soft snowy landing.
Snow Goose smooths her fine feathers.
"Let me help,"
she says.

And she pats down the snow
with her wide, webbed feet.

There's
splintering and splashing
coming from the icy lake.

Moose nuzzles the little white cub
with his velvet muzzle.
"Let me help," he says.
And he shovels more snow with his sweeping antlers.

There's
skidding and sliding
and the sound of
claws on ice.

Fox twitches her
frisky whiskers.
"Let me help,"
she says.

And she shapes the feet
  with her quick, curved claws.

There's
panting and pawing
and a lot of tail-wagging.
Wolf sniffs the air with his long, sharp nose.
"Let me help," he says.
And he brushes in the fur marks
with his big, bushy tail.

There's hopping and
stopping and
two long ears flopping.
Hare stares with
dark, liquid eyes.

"Let me help," she says.
And she draws the
face with her neat,
narrow paws.

Bear, Hare, and Wolf,
  Snow Goose and Moose,
    Musk Ox and Fox
finish the snow bear just as the sun
sets and the world is washed gold.
    But listen!

From the forest, their mothers
call them home—all except
for the little white bear's.
"Good-bye," he says sadly, as they
disappear into the dusk.
"Thank you for your help."

Darkness settles over the clearing.
The little white cub snuggles up against the
snow bear, wishing it were already morning.

As he sleeps, warm winds
blow from the south and
soften the snow.
Slowly, slowly, the snow bear
melts into the green of the forest.

But listen!

As dawn breaks, who comes
sniffing and searching
through the trees?

In the clearing, a new day begins.
A familiar scent awakens
the little white bear.
He blinks sleepily.
"It's you!" he murmurs,
moving closer to
his mother's side.
"I knew you would find me."

ISBN 0-439-38589-X

Text copyright © 2000 by Miriam Moss.
Illustrations copyright © 2000 by The Templar Company plc.
All rights reserved.
Published by Scholastic Inc., 557 Broadway, New York, NY 10012,
by arrangement with Dutton Children's Books, a member of Penguin Putnam Inc.
SCHOLASTIC and associated logos are trademarks
and/or registered trademarks of Scholastic Inc.

12 11 10   8/0

Printed in the U.S.A.   23

First Scholastic printing, January 2003